FRANK IN TIME

ROD CLEMENT

FRANK IN TIME

Angus&Robertson

An imprint of HarperCollins*Children's Books*

Every morning is an adventure for me, a journey of discovery.
Finding clean clothes isn't enough, I want more.

So today I'm going to travel in time and explore the past.
I don't mean looking at faded photos of your
grandparents or searching for the old sandwich
under the bed — I mean the really old stuff.

Travelling in time is not as hard as you think.
All you need is a backpack, good walking shoes
and two tickets to the museum.

Yes folks, the museum.
There's more old stuff in that place than you will ever find
in your attic or down the crack in the lounge!

Walking through the front door is like walking into history.
The first thing you see is a skeleton of a man standing next
to a skeleton of a dinosaur. They look like they're
going for a stroll.

The dinosaur must be well trained.

I wonder if he goes to obedience classes like Frank?

In the first display is a sculpture of the Ice age. It looks just like the inside of our freezer.

Perhaps the same scientists who found the frozen woolly mammoth could look for the ham and pineapple pizza we lost a few years ago.

Did you know that primitive man was covered in hair
and made tools out of stone?

Just imagine if all your tools were made of stone
— the tool kits must have weighed a ton!

They obviously couldn't make scissors out of stone — the hairstyles were terrible.

Egyptians were different — they cared about their appearance.
In fact they cared so much about their looks, they wanted to keep
them forever, even after they died!

That's why all the mummies
were wrapped up in
bandages — to protect
their skin.

I wonder where all the daddies were?
If they were anything like my dad they were probably all back
in the pyramids watching sport on TV.

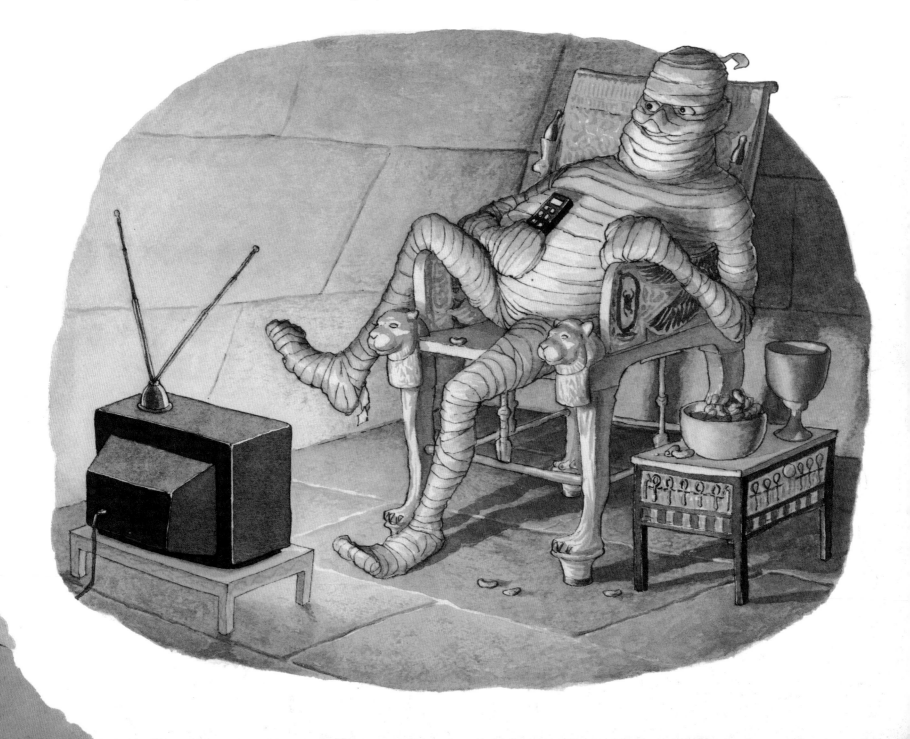

The Romans loved sport so much they built one of the earliest stadiums, the amphitheatre. Thousands of spectators would sit in the stands and cheer as their favourite gladiators fought to the death.

They were a bit like our quiz shows — if you won you got to come back next week.

People didn't go out much in the Middle Ages, it was too dangerous.

They spent most of the time locked up in their castles,

often with a moat and drawbridge

for extra protection.

It's a pity we don't have that extra protection now — it would make it so much easier to avoid door to door salesmen.

Finding things was a full-time job for Christopher Columbus. He sailed halfway round the world to find America and he didn't even have the address.

I wish he was alive today — he could sail halfway round the world again and find Mum's car keys.

You don't have to be on the move to discover things.
Isaac Newton was hit on the head by an apple while sitting
under a tree and discovered gravity.

Lucky he wasn't sitting under a coconut tree
— he could have been seriously hurt.

When Isaac Newton was explaining how gravity makes things fall
to the ground, I don't think Wilbur and Orville Wright were listening.
They spent most of their time trying to get off the ground and stay off.

After a lot of practice they managed to stay off the ground
for 59 seconds, which is about the same as my
record-breaking paper plane flight.

If they had used my design all they would have needed was a huge piece of paper and an enormous hand.

Once people learnt to fly there was no stopping them.

Getting off the ground wasn't enough — they wanted to get to the moon.

They went all that way to leave a flag and some footprints.

That's a long way to go just to make some footprints. It would have been a lot easier just to make them in the cement path that runs down our street.

So here we are back where we started after exploring
12,000 years of history. It wasn't too hard
— no scratches, bruises or serious illness
and still half a block of chocolate left.

It's great to know how things have changed and how people changed them. Anyone can change things if they try hard enough — even Frank.

So how can I make history?

'That's easy,' said my dad, 'you could be the first kid in the world
to do his homework and keep his room tidy.'

I agree. That's why I've decided to design and build
the world's first automatic room tidier.
Tidy the room — then the world!

Angus&Robertson
An imprint of HarperCollins*Children'sBooks*, Australia

First published in Australia in 1998
This Bluegum paperback edition first published in 1999
by HarperCollins*Publishers* Australia Pty Limited
ABN 36 009 913 517
harpercollins.com.au

HarperCollins*Publishers*
Level 13, 201 Elizabeth Street, Sydney NSW 2000, Australia
Unit D1, 63 Apollo Drive, Rosedale, Auckland 0632, New Zealand
A 53, Sector 57, Noida, UP, India
1 London Bridge Street, London, SE1 9GF, United Kingdom
2 Bloor Street East, 20th floor, Toronto, Ontario M4W 1A8, Canada
195 Broadway, New York NY 10007, USA

National Library of Australia Cataloguing-in-Publication entry:

Clement, Rod.
Frank in Time.
ISBN: 978 0 207 19896 0
I. Title.
A823.3

Colour reproduction by Graphic Print Group, Adelaide, South Australia
Printed by RR Donnelley in China, on 128gsm Matt Art

6 5 4 3   16 17 18 19